Amish Romance

The Amish Reunion:
A New Beginning

Jocelin Hewish

The

Amish Reunion

A New Beginning

Jocelin Hewish

The boy who came back

She was 20 that day they met each other under the maple tree that blossomed with wide branches beside the baker's house. He was there with a group of friends, other young boys like him who worked at the sawmill where they produced wooden cabinets, chairs and dressing tables, each of them working with the hopes of earning enough money to help support their families.

It had been a cloudy September evening, one of those quiet days she had expected nothing from the world, nothing that could excite her enough to change her life as she knew it. But when it had happened, as she beheld his eyes that day walking by the laughing boys with their handsaws and hammers, she knew it. Even four months later, she still couldn't tell what had been so mesmerizing, so captivating about his charm. Of course she knew him. Every other girl in her age grade knew his name and whispered it in their sleep. It was a guilty pleasure they all enjoyed, something they all knew was definitely devilish, but then it controlled them so much they gave in so effortlessly.

It was from Pearl she had first heard his name. His story had flowed out effortlessly from Pearl's mouth like something she had memorized off a book. Pearl told her that she had lived close to his family when she was little, around the same time he had been taken out of the community by some English people to join a baseball team. Since that time Pearl had never set her eyes on him again, until when he returned to the community around a year ago.

Amity could still remember that night when Pearl had told her the whole story. She still remembered how her friend's eyeballs had glowed whenever she mentioned his name. In their over-ten years of friendship she had never seen Pearl that excited about a person, except for when her mother had given birth to a baby boy who they had sadly lost to a mysterious sickness that confounded local doctors and went without a solution. It was the end of his story that had totally broken Amity, when Pearl revealed to her his main reason for returning to the community and losing his place at the team. It had been an injury to his heel which left him leaping around on crutches. His speed and stamina had suffered and the team had decided that they needed him no more. *They used the milk and disposed the useless container,* was how Pearl had summarized the story.

Even though Amity had never set her eyes on this boy who they called Levi, she was able to create a picture of him in her mind that night before bed, once she had taken her bath and tried to put her body to rest. The problem was that rest remained far from her mind throughout the night. She was tormented till the morning came. An imaginary face, fully formed by the machinations of her mind floated around in her head. She'd found herself weeping softly, tears that tasted of pity. She pitied this Levi boy so much, imagining all he must have had to go through since the club decided they had had enough of him.

She that boys, even the Amish ones, always pretended to be strong even when they needed help, especially after going through a private torture like the one that Levi had been through. They all did that for the sake of their masculinity, pretend to be well even though they were gradually dying inside. She was sure that this boy was going through this and she wished she could help him out in any way possible.

With all of this, it was quite easy to understand why Amity didn't find it hard identifying him among the group of other boys once she set her eyes on him. He fit all of the descriptions that Pearl had given: there was his terrifying height that helped him stand taller than all of the other boys, his limping gait and the dimples that hovered on his cheeks when he smiled. It was all there. All Amity had to do was to ignore him and fix her gaze on the tarred road to ensure that she never gave off the impression that she liked the fact that his gaze lingered on her as she walked by.

She never got to see him again until the next week at the church. He was sitting there at the other side of the hall. Pearl was there, too, sitting by her side with her bible in her hands. That Sunday morning, Amity noticed a difference in Pearl. Her friend had become so consumed by his charm on this day, more consumed than she had ever been before. It bothered Amity, but she knew there was nothing she could do. She simply kept her gaze to the front of the hall, taking in the words that flowed from the preacher mouth, asking that *Gott filled her with them.*

Once the service was over, Amity moved over to the back of the church, to the small building that they used for the children Sunday school. Most of the children knew her and once they saw her they ran towards her and wrapped their arms around her, exclaiming her name in loud tones. Amity gave each of them a warm embrace and picked a few off the ground to coo them. She then sat with them, telling Bible stories, as she waited for Pearl to arrive with the brooms. It was a job left for the two girls. They were to clean the children church once each Sunday service was over. As usual, this always came with a little chit-chat to pass away the time. Today would turn out to be totally different, more different than Amity could have imagined.

Pearl arrived with a beam glowing allover her face and her smile as wide as the Heavens.

"I saw him! I saw him! I saw just saw him!" Pearl's voice rang through the small room, and it seemed to Amity like she could feel the chairs vibrate under it turbulence. For a while she stepped aside and allowed Pearl a moment to relieve all of the excitement building up and swelling in her as she galloped lightly like a young stallion. Soon she came to halt and looked into Amity's eyes still bearing a glowing smile in her eyes. Amity looked at her and something hit her: Pearl was really beautiful. She had never complimented her before, but she knew that the time would come for that soon.

"Okay, okay…" Amity began teasingly, "I am happy you saw him, but so what? What do we do with that information? Will it help us out in milking the cows or baking the bread?" She couldn't tell when those words dropped from her mouth. She had not want to sound this unpleased, but then this Levi of a boy had consumed too much of their lives and all she wanted was a little release for the both of them. Even as she considered this inwardly, she knew she was only dreaming. It would take *Gott's* grace and power to liberate the two friends from this entanglement.

Pearl fixed a piecing look on her face. She too had been confounded by such a statement coming from Amity. This defiance was unfounded. So unlike the Amity she knew. "Are you serious, right now?" She asked. "Why did you have to say that?"

Amity kept her mouth shut. She didn't even have an answer for Pearl. As the both them stood there looking into each other's eyes, she wished time would rush by and help them pass through this moment without more interaction about this topic. Something hit her, something that could help lighten the moment for a little while.

"Where are the brooms? You have brought none?"

Pearl looked down to her hands and discovered what Amity was saying. She had been so consumed with the gleeful emotion, with the sight of Levi, that her mind had lost grip of reality and fluttered off leaving her with a blank space in her mind where nothing really mattered. She bit her lips and scolded herself inwardly for her mistake. This would mean her walking back to the store to pick up the brooms. She and Amity had faced this problem many times where they would be the last to reach the store and meet all the brooms taken off by the other girls who had been assigned to sweep the church or its compound.

Amity stifled a giggle. "Okay, you will have to go back and get those brooms. If you find them all gone, you come back and we see what we can do. And please don't allow that young man distract you this time."

"I wasn't distracted by him. I was..." Amity could see that words had failed her friend.

"You were what?" She asked and allowed Pearl a moment to search her mind for an answer. Obviously, there was none. The two of them knew this.

"I will be back," Pearl said, making a smooth turned while standing on her heels, "and this time I promise not to be distracted like a dog."

Amity gave her a small, encouraging tap on her back and reassured her, "You are not a dog, dear." The both of them shared a laugh as Pearl walked off out of the children church.

Alone, Amity began rearranging the chairs that the little ones had now scattered during their play time. She noticed that the chairs had been changed recently, their current wooden design quite an improvement on the former chairs that she had used as a child in the Sunday school. Her mind presented her with fragmented images of the time before she clocked fourteen, those days when she knew nothing about anything. Being the last one among five children, she could say that she had grown up spoilt and pampered, but not in the way the English children were pampered with Barbie dolls and Saturday morning sitcoms. Her own had come basically from her four elder siblings who always did all the house chores even before she was awake. It was after they started growing into adults and leaving the house to go be with their husbands and wives that the reality of life had started dawning on her. It was at this time that Amity had started learning how to milk the cows or bake bread. Now she was a full grown woman who would be ready to leave her parent's house soon and go be with her new husband. The thought pinched her in her mind as she pushed off the last chair to the corner to make space for the sweeping.

Just then she heard footsteps and knew that Pearl was approaching. All she wanted to do was get home and dig into the muffins and warm milk her mother had prepared earlier that morning and then have some time to rest her head before the next morning.

She felt a shadow land on her body and wondered why Pearl would reach the door and just remain there. Had she not found any of the brooms? She turned back to look and see what was happening there at the door, but her eyes were accosted by the most unfamiliar and unexpected sight ever. Where she had expected to see a gown flowing down to a woman's feet, she saw a demarcation between the legs that signified trousers. The shock caused her to move her head upwards to see the face. Oh, how she lost her breath and missed consecutive heartbeats. Levi. Levi. Levi. It was Levi.

A new friend

To say that Amity was shocked would be an understatement. She was literally drowning in it. It was evident in all of the goosebumps that found root on her skin and rose to make themselves more evident. The dryness in her throat spread from its base almost the top of her mouth and she knew something had to be done before she fooled herself even more. The first words she released tumbled out of her lips with a stammer.

"Good day, I am… You are…" She needed to take a deep breath as quickly as possible or she would end up ruining this moment. Maybe she wanted it ruined, though. It would be too hard to get it right and sustain the momentum. She no longer cared. What she did was to prepare her most serious countenance and plaster it across her face.

"Well done, Sir. Are you looking for someone?"

Now she wondered why he hadn't even talked. If he came for something he could have asked for it and moved along, instead of standing there and make all of this seem so weird and awkward.

Even his voice seemed like something from an angelic dream, a pure fantasy to her ears. If only she could bottle it up and save it in her room, on her small wooden table that bore nothing other than her night lamp and her bible. She imagined herself opening up this bottle each night and listening to his voice fill up the room while she slept.

"Your friend told me you would be here. I just wanted to talk to you. That's all."

Amity could feel the ground shift under her feet. There was an earthquake happening inside of her and only his voice could help her, but she told herself she needed to resist this help.

Levi worsened this inner commotion by walking towards her. She could perceive his dense and manly smell that consisted of hardworking sweat as it filled the air that existed between him and her. She felt something invisible push her from behind towards him and she imagined herself finally end up in his strong arms. It all happened in her head as she knew better than to ever allow that happen in real life.

When he reached her, Amity knew it was all over. She had lost. She hadn't been able to say anything to counter his last words.

"Your friend, Pearl, Pearl Abraham. I asked about you and she told me you were in here."

"You know me? Are you sure you aren't mistaking me for someone else? Because I don't know you myself."

"You don't know me? Really? Actually, I know you quite well. We spent most of childhood Sundays in this hall." Levi used his hand to gesticulate the space that they were now confined in.

Amity had never imagined this. She had never been able to put any of this into perspective, to ever think that she had grown up with Levi. But now, as she listened to him, it dawned on her that he could have a point. He had been part of her childhood and she had missed him. She looked into his eyes questioningly. It wasn't a question for him, but a question for their past, a searching to find a viable connection.

"I know your brother, Jude, the one that had the accident when he was sixteen."

Something struck Amity as she heard these words and memories came rushing back into her mind. Yes, it was true. Jude, her second brother and the second child of her parents, had been in an accident some years back, on a rainy night when a horse had lost control and taken the buggy into a ditch. She still remembered the night Jude had returned home from the hospital after days of being there, their mother going over to see him and spend each night with him. It had been a dark time in their home, and even up till this moment, even though she was supposed to have grown past that dark time just like everyone else in her family, Amity was still plagued by the sounds of her brother's screams that had filled the house those nights when the doctor came over to stretch his bones. She never wanted to be associated with that memory ever again in her life, but in this situation, since it was Levi that had dragged her down into it, she was willing to take the chance.

"How is he doing now?" Levi asked. "I left to join my baseball team within weeks of that accident. I wasn't able to gather up enough information about how well he fared once I left the community."

It was at this time that Amity remembered the stories Pearl had relayed to her about Levi's predicament: his injury and the abandonment of his former baseball team. Amity knew she would have to chip that into their conversation to fill up holes and avoid any awkward silences, something she truly detested when talking to anybody.

"He is better now. It has been years since and he is married now. You could have seen him during the service if you looked well enough."

"Really? He is married now?" Levi exclaimed.

"Of course, he is." She could not explain this sudden excitement that had now clouded his face. The news of a marriage had gotten his face filled up with the contours of multiple smiles. She knew that he too yearned to be a husband, to be a father and to have children run around his home and call him '*daed*'. She wished that *Gott* would grant him this heart desire. "How is your leg? Pearl told me about the injury. I hope you are doing better now?"

"Pearl told you that?" he asked, with an alarm in his face that made Amity think he didn't want anybody to know this story.

"Yes, she did. I am sorry if this offends…"

"No, it doesn't…only that you just claimed not to know me."

It was blow to Amity's face. She had lied and Levi had discovered it. She needed to find a way to redeem herself.

For a few seconds, in the moment of silence that engulfed them, Levi looked down to his feet and Amity wondered what he was thinking, it had been wrong for her to ask him that question.

"All I can say is that *Gott* was there for me when I needed him the most. He was faithful even when the team decided to fail me. He showed me his mercy."

Amity nodded in agreement as she tried to take away her gaze from his brown eyes that were at the verge of drowning her.

Just then, Pearl arrived with the brooms. She stopped there at the door and pretended like she had interrupted something. Amity thought she noticed a disappointment in her face, a disappointment she felt wouldn't have existed if Pearl had been the one Levi was in conversation with.

"Oh, I see you have found her," Pearl said.

Levi turned and nodded. "Yes, Pearl. All thanks to you. And we just finished having a nice chat about a lot of things. I should get going and go see my father. Pretty sure he would have an errand for me right now."

Amity watched as he pulled backwards and nodded at the both of them. "I will see you girls later," he said as his head disappeared behind the door.

He didn't even let Amity catch her breath before he returned. "Amity, will you be free tomorrow? I would love to have some more time with you. That's if you would love to."

Amity took in a deep and long breath. She could feel Pearl's stare boring into her soul as the question hung in the air. For a long time, she contemplated her dilemma. She knew that Pearl would give anything to be in her shoes right now, to be the one contemplating this particular question. Now she was stuck between the angry Egyptians and the big Red Sea. If she refused this proposal it would mean losing Levi forever. If she accepted, she didn't know how Pearl would react.

"Sure. I will be free in the afternoon. My mother won't need my help anymore at that time. Where would you want us to meet?"

It was a reply that had jumped out by itself, a reply that had formed on its own in her mind and found a way to come out into the world to grace the occasion. She wouldn't dare look to see what was happening on Pearl face at that moment. All she did then was to concentrate her mind on Levi and the smile that had blanketed his face. She could tell that he would do anything just to be with her and talk about their lives.

"I will be at the park. 5pm tomorrow. See you there then." And with that the young man left the two women standing there drowned in silence.

Their eyes met and Pearl was the first to break the silence.

"Wow! He likes you. He really does."

No matter how much Pearl tried to mask the pain that littered her voice, Amity was able to figure out its existence even as she handed her the broom and the both of them got down to start sweeping the hall.

The Meeting

It was the same manly smell, exactly like the one that had assaulted her nose the day before in the children section of the church. Even now as she tried to imagine all that had transpired between her, Pearl and Levi, she could feel a kind of feverish excitement growing on her skin. After cleaning up the room and dusting all of the chairs, Pearl had excused herself and walked out to get something whose name Amity had been unable to gather since Pearl had muttered her words under her breath. Unfortunately, she never returned and Amity had had to walk home alone, the first time this had happened in years. Throughout that day she hadn't even come across Pearl. She was confused even though her mind tried to present her with reasons why Pearl had avoided throughout the day. She desperately didn't want to believe that Pearl had avoided her because of that conversation with Levi the day before.

She caught sight of him seating alone in the park. That evening there were no children hanging around and playing hide-and-seek. No frustrated mothers yelling and asking them not to stain their gowns or shirts. The park was calm, so calm that Amity felt she could feel a portion of it entering her heart and filling up her soul. Nobody could resist Levi. He had that charm, that calmness that easier spread around him and encapsulated his environment.

She had noticed him as he had his gaze afar off, towards the road where a black buggy was being pulled by a stallion. She could hear the noise the four wheels made as they rolled repeated over the tarred road. She imagined the residents of that buggy, imagined what their lives would be like and all she wanted to do was to tell them that she was happy. She was calm, and that she now had Levi.

Levi's gaze fell on her as she approached. He still appeared a little bit distant and but his smile could not be mistaken for anything else. Underneath his hands, and Amity could sense that he was trying to hide this stuff, was something that looked like a brown paper bag. Amity's stomach rumbled gently as the strong, inviting aroma of glazed doughnuts swung over and around her nose.

"I didn't think you'd come." Levi said, adjusting himself on the seat to make way for her.

The evening was cool, and the sky lacked a single cloud. Everything above their heads was blue and Amity was thankful to simply be alive.

She avoided his eyes and made to tie up the knots of her shoes, although they were both perfectly in place. "Why did you think so? I made a promise. A promise made is trust on the line. I have my integrity to uphold, you know."

Levi nodded. "I understand all of that, but still...sometimes, you know. People still ignore the 'integrity' clause and fail others." He used his finger to indicate the presence of quotation marks over the word 'integrity'. "It is quite understandable that not everyone will turn out this way, but, you know, I have to be careful. I don't want to get hurt twice. Life has already dealt me a blow."

Those words revived Amity's attention. They were only minutes into their conversation but he was already plunging them into unexplainable depths. She felt uncomfortable, yet knew that there would be no easy way out. Just as she had prayed and asked *Gott* to allow her help out Levi, *Gott* had answered her prayer and brought her to him. She was going to be a vessel in his hands and she made a mental note in her mind not to fail him. But, first, she wanted him to explain, to tell her what he meant by, *I don't want to get hurt twice.*

"You don't want to be hurt again? How do you mean?" Her words were like a spear, she could tell. They pierced deep into Levi's heart and generate a fresh wound of truth. He didn't want to talk about it, but he needed to. He needed to heal and the best way to do that would be to start talking and letting out of the pain.

For a few seconds, Levi kept his gaze away from her face. This time he looked to his right, the side of him that faced the larger part of the field before it stopped at the road that led to the carpentry workshop that had been built by an English man. Amity thought she could hear the slightest sob in his voice, stifled and suppressed but still there.

"It was my coach, I trusted him." Levi's voice gave and he feel down into the sorrow that was clouding his voice and heart. He sobbed for a little while and then used the back of his hands to rub off the tears that had gathered underneath his eyes while backing Amity throughout. Then he turned to her to reveal reddened eyes.

Amity placed her hands briefly on his and she felt the warm follow of faith cruise from her palms into his. It was the least she could do to encourage him as best as possible. She hoped it was working, because she could sense that Levi needed all the support he could get at this time.

"When they discovered my talent and came to pick me up, they had lots of promises. And I fell for all of them. I didn't look at what Gott wanted. All I had my eyes on were on the things I wanted. I saw the fame. I saw the money, I saw the enjoyments that would come with living with the English people and mingling with them. I guess the Devil was having a swell time and laughing at me as I gradually walked into his trap"

He paused for a while and shook his head in regret. "I was really foolish. If only I had used my senses, I could have seen all of it coming."

"It wasn't your fault." Amity said. It was all she knew to say to help him feel better. "I am happy you have discovered your mistake and that you are ready to make adjustments. I want you to know that Gott himself is always ready to let you back into his flock. I want you to always remember that."

Levi nodded as she spoke, her words piercing deeper and deeper into him. He had truly never had anyone confront his past in this comforting way before. After his return to the community, it had been months of rebuke and corrections from his father who had never wanted to see him leave in the first place. No one had ever tried to offer words of advice to him. Here was a girl he had only met within the space of thirty-six hours and it already felt like he could place his life on her shoulder.

"I am sorry to be burdening you with so much from my past. I shouldn't be doing this. I have only just met you." Levi said.

"Stop apologizing for anything. This is why we are a community. We are supposed to support and help each other out in times like this. Like I said before, I am only lucky to be a vessel in *Gott's* hands. I only want to see the best for you." Amity tried to assure him, toning down her voice so as not to sound too harsh and push him off.

"I can't appreciate you enough for this. All of my friends aren't this connected with me in a deep way. All we do is laugh and play, but no one is ready to help me bear my burden as friends should. Anyway, as they say, 'Boys will always be boys'."

The two of them burst in a mild laughter at the sound of that and then they stopped. For a while they remained silent, but it was a comfortable silence, one needed to help them process their environment and make new mental registrations.

"It is getting late. I should get going to help my mother out with her chores. She would be needing me anytime soon. I am really sorry we won't be able to see each other for too long today. I really wish we could have that time to ourselves. Are you leaving anytime soon?"

"Yes, yes. I am leaving too. I would really love to see you off, but I need to get to the market and get a few supplies." He said, slipping the brown envelope into her hand. "This is for you."

"You didn't need to bother yourself."

"I understand. I know. I only decided I didn't want our first meeting as friends to be without a gift, no matter how small. It is the least I can do considering how much you did for me this evening, coming over at such short notice."

Amity smiled and took the brown paper bag from him. "It smells nice. I am also sure it tastes really good. Thank you for this. Finally have something to sneak into my room this night."

"You sure do. I am glad you have accepted my small gift. Thank you for this."

***

Amity could see him walking off as he turned off into the part that lead that lead to the market. Even from this distance, she could sense the glee that had clouded Levi face, could feel the sorrow that had been lifted off his heart. It gladdened her, but something else bother her. It was Pearl.

The Story Continues